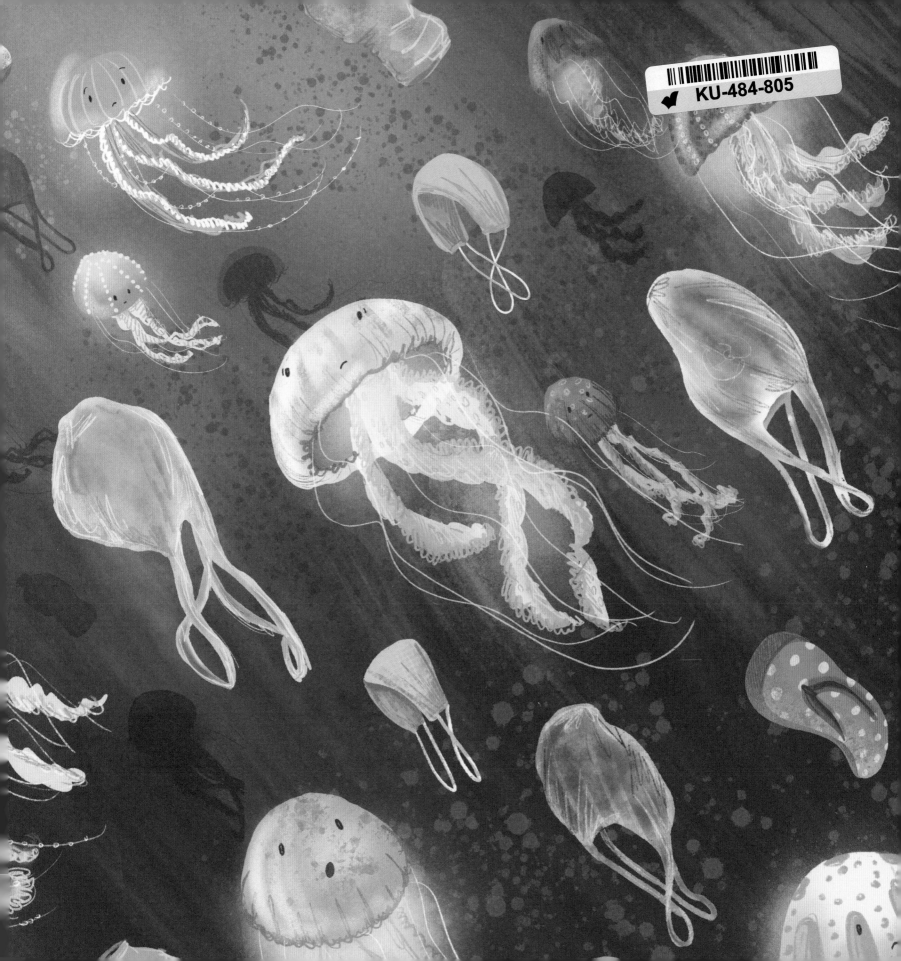

For Andy, Joseph, Amalie, Mum, and Dad

Published by Sunbird Books, an imprint of Phoenix International Publications, Inc.

8501 West Higgins Road   34 Seymour Street   Heimhuder Straße 81
Chicago, Illinois 60631   London W1H 7JE   20148 Hamburg

www.sunbirdkidsbooks.com

Text and illustrations © 2022 Julia Seal

Library of Congress Control Number: 2021941103

ISBN: 978-1-5037-6495-8 Printed in China

Text set in Chelsea Market Pro.

BLOOM

Written and illustrated by Julia Seal

sunbird books

There was a time when the
ocean was full of friends.

Colourful friends...

helpful friends...

FULL CLEAN
TEETH ONLY
CLEAN & POLISH

friends who liked to play chase.

There was a perfect rhythm to the waves and a perfect balance to the water.

Luna loved to roam the sea, but she always came back to her friends at the reef. Everyone wanted to hear her stories about things she had seen...

like jet skis...

and armbands...

and castles made of sand.

They all listened with wonder, especially her best friend Hermit, who had never been far from home.

Lately, Luna noticed
that things were changing.

"Look at my fabulous new shell!"

"What an unusual flavour!"

"Is it getting hot in here, or is it just me?"

And when Luna returned to the reef after her next adventure...

Hermit and her other friends were gone! So she set off to find them.

Luna asked some strange-looking fish if they'd seen her friends, but they just floated by.

She asked a pair of quiet jellyfish...

but they didn't have much to say.

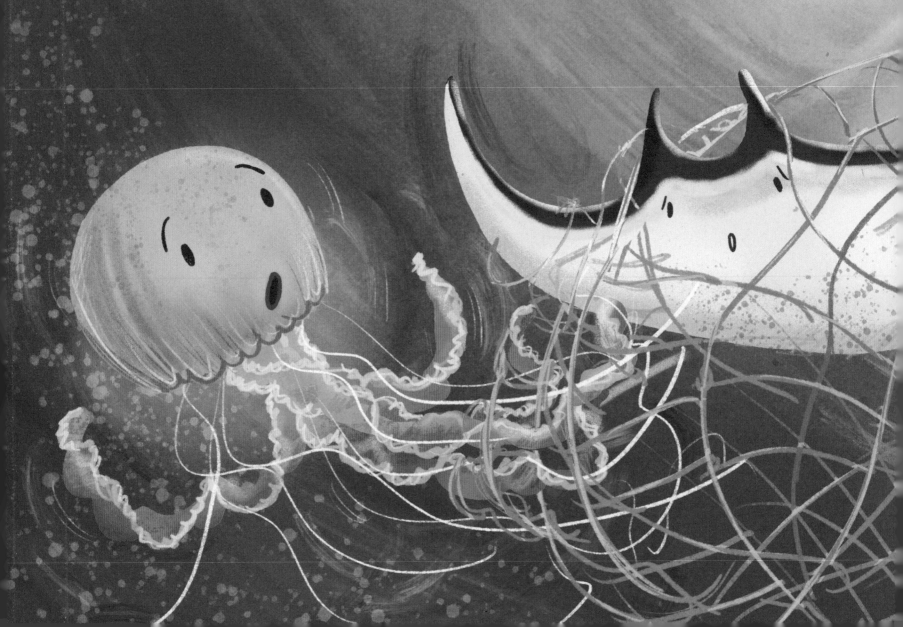

She tried to question some manta rays, but they were too busy to help.

Just as Luna was giving up hope, she saw something bright in the distance.

A huge **BLOOM** of jellyfish!

"I've lost my friends!" Luna said. "Will you help me find them?"
The bloom of jellyfish spread out to look, and before long they
reached the reef.

As their tentacles brushed over the cluttered seabed, there was a rustle in the plastic. Luna's heart jumped for joy as Hermit crawled out, camouflaged by his new shell.

"The ocean is in trouble," said Hermit.

"The waters are warming, and the waves are carrying things that don't belong here. We need to do something."
     Luna wanted to help her friend. But what could one little jellyfish do?

All the things Luna
had seen had rippled back
to the reef, upsetting the
perfect balance.

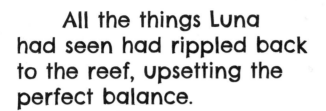

She gazed at the
hundreds of jellyfish
swimming around her...and
suddenly had an answer.

One little jellyfish can't do much,
but a huge BLOOM of jellyfish can!

So together, the jellyfish turned up by the beaches.

They blocked up power stations.

They weighed down fishing nets, nearly overturning the boats! Their silent message was loud and clear...

In recent years, our oceans have seen huge blooms of jellyfish, unlike ever before. Jellyfish thrive in rising sea temperatures, acidic water, and pollution. They are known as an indicator species, because their increased presence is a warning sign that something is out of balance in our oceans.

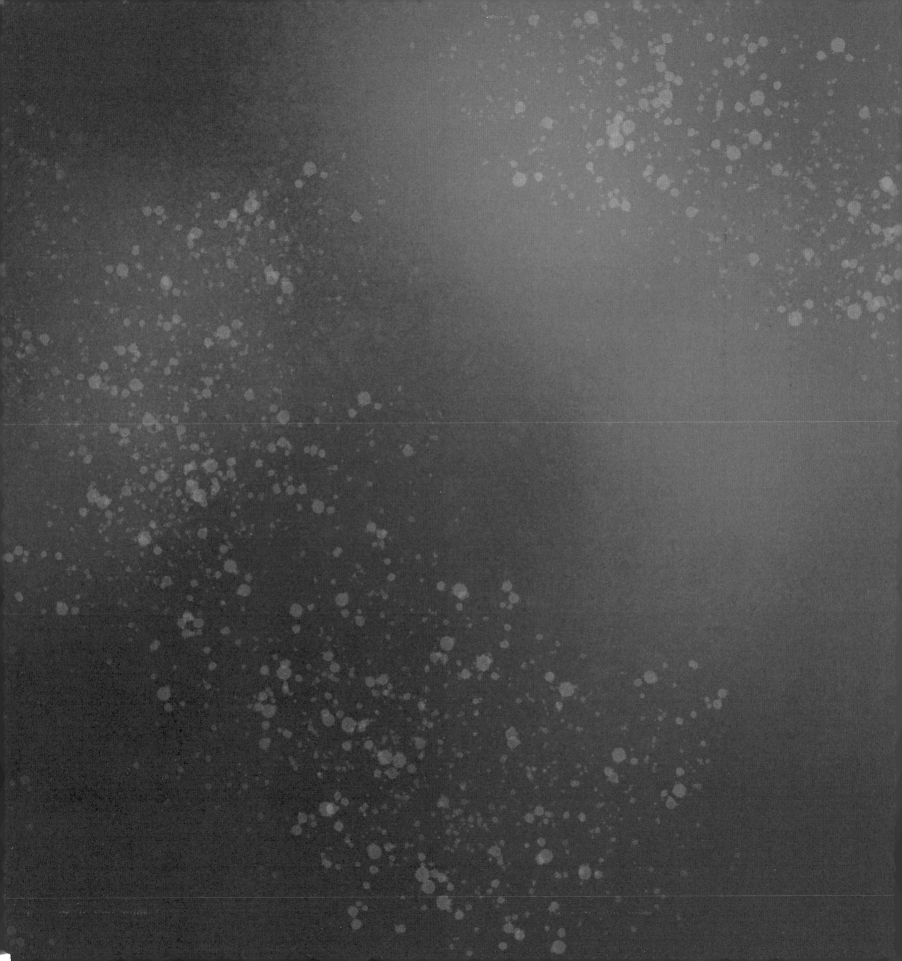